This book belongs to

Amber

Thumper

Bambi

STARRING

Flower

The
Great
Prince

This edition published by Parragon in 2010

Parragon
Queen Street House
4 Queen Street
Bath, BA1 1HE, UK

ISBN 978-1-4075-8761-5
Printed in China

Bath · New York · Singapore · Hong Kong · Cologne · Delhi · Melbourne

One spring morning, there was great excitement in the forest. A new Prince had been born. His name was Bambi. He was the son of a noble stag, the Great Prince of the Forest.

Bambi lay asleep by his mother's side. When he woke, the littl[e] spotted fawn saw happy smiling faces all around him.

"My name's Thumper," said a friendly rabbit. Bambi smiled.

It wasn't long before Bambi was ready to explore the forest. He made lots of new friends.

"The forest is a
wonderful place!"
Bambi thought to
himself.

One day, Bambi and Thumper were playing. Birds fluttered above their heads. Thumper pointed at one and said, "That's a bird."

Bambi repeated the word, "Bird!"

Then a butterfly fluttered by. Bambi called out, "Bird!"

"No," giggled Thumper, "that's a butterfly."

Bambi turned to a pretty flower and shouted, "Butterfly!"

Thumper laughed. "No," he cried, "that's a flower!"

Bambi bent down to smell the flowers. Suddenly, a small black and white head popped up from under the petals.

"Flower!" said Bambi, again.

"That's not a flower, that's a skunk!"
Thumper laughed.

"He can call me Flower if he wants to," said
the little skunk.

Bambi had made
another new friend.

The days passed happily for Bambi. One morning his mother took him to a new place—the meadow.

The meadow was wide and open. Bambi's mother warned him that they had to be very careful. "There are no trees here to hide us," she said.

Bambi ran off to play. Soon, he found a pond. He leaned over and looked into the water at his own reflection. Suddenly, another reflection appeared. It belonged to a female fawn about the same age as Bambi. She wanted to play.

Bambi felt very shy, and ran back to his mother.
"It's all right," Bambi's mother said. "That's
aline. She just wants to be your friend. Go
nd say hello."
Bambi went back to Faline. When she
egan to chase him, Bambi chased her.
oon, the two fawns were playing
de-and-seek in the
ll grass.

Just then, a group of stags charged across the meadow, led by the Great Prince. He had come to warn the deer that there wo danger nearby.

As the deer dashed towards the trees, Bambi couldn't find hi mother. He began to panic. The next moment his father was beside him.

Bambi followed the Great Prince into the forest and was overjoyed to see his mother there too.

Later that day, Bambi asked his mother what the dang had been.

"Man was in the forest," she told him.

Summer and autumn passed and the weather grew colder.

One morning, Bambi woke up to find the world had turned white. Bambi's mother saw his surprise.

"That's snow," she said. "Winter has come."

Bambi was having great fun making hoof prints in the snow, when he heard Thumper calling him.

Bambi found his friend sliding across an icy pond.

"The water's stiff," called Thumper. "Come on, you can slide too!"

Bambi rushed over to join him. But he
[fe]l on his tummy with a
[lo]ud—THUD!
Thumper showed
[B]ambi how to balance on
[th]e ice. Soon, Bambi was
[gli]ding across the
[po]nd too!

Winter was fun at first but, as time passed by, there was less and less food. All the animals grew hungry.

Eventually, there was nothing for Bambi and his mother to ea except the bark on the trees.

One day, when it felt a little warmer, Bambi and his mother went to the meadow to search for food. There they found a small patch of green grass peeping out of the snow.

Bambi and his mother ate the grass hungrily.

ıddenly, Bambi's mother looked up and sniffed the air. She
ınsed danger.

"Go back to the forest!" she ordered Bambi. "Quickly! Run!"
Bambi raced across the meadow with his mother behind him.
here was a loud—**BANG!**

"Faster, Bambi, and don't look back!" his mother shouted.
Bambi ran on to the forest, where it was safe.

Home at last, Bambi turned to look for his mother. But she was not there.

Bambi's heart thumped with panic. He called for his mother again and again. The little fawn began to cry.

Just then, his father appeared by his side.

"Your mother cannot be with you
~~ny~~ longer," he told Bambi gently.
~~~he~~ Great Prince would now protect his son until he
~~~uld~~ look after himself.
~~~As~~ the months passed, Bambi and his friends grew up.

One day, Flower met a female skunk and fell in love.

"Oh, no!" said Thumper. "Flower's twitterpated! Owl says it happens to everyone in the springtime!"

"It won't happen to me," Bambi said.

"Me neither," Thumper agreed.

Minutes later, Thumper met a female rabbit and he too was twitterpated.

Bambi wandered off for a drink.

"Hello," said a soft voice. It was Faline, his childhood friend.

Faline licked Bambi's face. He liked it. He'd become twitterpated too!

But another young stag called Ronno also liked Faline. He challenged Bambi to a fight. Although Ronno was stronger, Bambi won. Bambi and Faline were free to begin their life together.

One autumn morning, Bambi was woken by a strange smell. He left Faline sleeping and went to investigate.

He climbed a cliff and saw smoke in the distance. Just then, his
ther came up beside him.
"Man has returned," he said. "We must go deep into the
forest—quickly!"

Bambi rushed to warn Faline.
A pack of angry dogs had her
trapped on a
cliff.

Bambi rushed at the dogs and Faline escaped. Bambi fought them off and turned to follow Faline. Suddenly, he heard a loud—
BANG!

He felt a terrible pain and fell to the ground.
Flames from man's campfire swept towards Bambi but he could
ot move. The forest was on fire.
"Get up, Bambi," a voice cried. It was Bambi's father.
The young Prince staggered to his feet and followed his father
hrough the burning forest. They came to a waterfall and
mped. Down and down they fell and crashed into the water
r below. Bambi and his father waded through the water and
eaded towards an island.

Many other birds and animals had already found shelter there
Faline was there too. She was overjoyed to see Bambi again and
gently licked his wounded shoulder.

Safe on the island, the forest creatures watched helplessly as
e fire destroyed their homes.
When the fire finally burned out, the animals returned to
e forest.

fter a long, hard winter, spring arrived.

v grass and flowers grew where the fire had been. The forest was

utiful once again.

ne warm morning, all the animals and birds came to see Faline

her two new fawns. Standing nearby was their proud father,

bi, the new Great Prince of the Forest.